WONDER WOMAN

You Choose Stories: Wonder Woman
is published by Stone Arch Books,
A Capstone Imprint
1710 Roe Crest Drive
North Mankato, Minnesota 56003
www.capstonepub.com

STAR41679

Library of Congress Cataloging-in-Publication Data is
available on the Library of Congress website.
ISBN: 978-1-4965-8348-2 (library binding)
ISBN: 978-1-4965-8438-0 (paperback)
ISBN: 978-1-4965-8353-6 (eBook PDF)

Summary: In the middle of a battle, Wonder Woman and
Giganta get dragged deep into the earth. They soon learn
that Hades, the Ruler of the Underworld, is bored. But he
can't decide if the Amazon warrior or the size-shifting
super-villain would make a better sparring partner. Rather
than fight for the right to battle him, Wonder Woman and
Giganta plot a path to freedom. Now it's up to you to help
them escape *The Heart of Hades!*

Editor: Christopher Harbo

Designer: Hilary Wacholz

Printed in the United States of America.
PA70

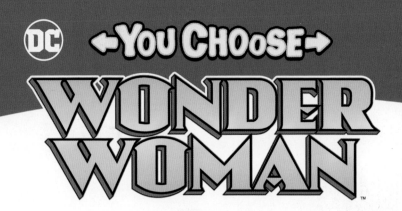

THE HEART OF HADES

written by
Laurie S. Sutton

illustrated by
Omar Lozano

Wonder Woman **created by**
William Moulton Marston

STONE ARCH BOOKS
a capstone imprint

←YOU CHOOSE→

WONDER WOMAN

In the middle of a battle, Wonder Woman and Giganta get dragged deep into the earth. They soon learn that Hades, the Ruler of the Underworld, is bored. But he can't decide if the Amazon warrior or the size-shifting super-villain would make a better sparring partner. Rather than fight for the right to battle him, Wonder Woman and Giganta plot a path to freedom. Now it's up to you to help them escape *The Heart of Hades!*

Follow the directions at the bottom of each page. The choices YOU make will change the outcome of the story. After you finish one path, go back and read the others for more Wonder Woman adventures!

Wonder Woman flies in her Invisible Jet high up in the clear blue sky. She likes watching the city pass below her feet through the see-through hull. Suddenly she sees something unusual. A giant woman is trying to stomp several police cars! The woman is twenty feet tall and holds an armored bank truck in one hand. The Amazon Princess recognizes the super-sized villain.

"Giganta!" Wonder Woman says.

Wonder Woman swoops the Invisible Jet down toward the action. **ZOOOOM!** She arrives just as Giganta shakes the truck's guards out of the vehicle. They fall toward the ground twenty feet below!

"Don't worry. I'll catch you!" Wonder Woman shouts.

Wonder Woman opens the roof of the cockpit and flies under the falling men. They tumble into the jet and land next to her. *THUMP! THUMP!*

Turn the page.

"Whew! Thank you, Wonder Woman!" the guards exclaim.

Wonder Woman lands her Invisible Jet and jumps out to meet Giganta head-on. The police officers step back when they see the super hero on the scene. As soon as Giganta spots Wonder Woman, she tries to stomp the Amazon Princess.

"You can't stop me," Giganta says. "I'll flatten you like a pancake."

Wonder Woman leaps aside and twirls her golden lasso. It catches Giganta around the ankle. Wonder Woman uses her incredible Amazonian strength to yank on the lasso and pull Giganta off balance. The super-villain tips over and crashes to the ground.

Suddenly the ground splits open! But it isn't Giganta's fall that causes the crack. An enormous black dog with three heads leaps out of the opening. Wonder Woman recognizes the creature instantly.

"Cerberus! The guard dog of the Underworld!" Wonder Woman gasps.

Cerberus hears his name and looks toward Wonder Woman. He lets out a loud bark and leaps at the Amazon. The giant hound is so fast that even Wonder Woman cannot dodge him in time. Cerberus grabs Wonder Woman in his jaws and jumps back down into the split in the earth. Giganta, who is still caught in Wonder Woman's lasso, gets dragged right along with her.

Cerberus carries Wonder Woman and Giganta down a shaft in the earth. In only a few moments they reach the bottom and land in front of a huge palace. A tall man in armor walks up to Cerberus and pats one of his heads.

"Good boy," the man says. Cerberus drops Wonder Woman.

"Hades!" Wonder Woman says as she wipes off dog drool.

"Hades? Like the God of the Dead?" Giganta asks, amazed.

"In the flesh," Hades replies. "I see Cerberus brought a hero *and* a villain to me. This is an unexpected bonus."

Turn the page.

"What do you want with us, Hades?" Wonder Woman asks.

"I'm bored and I want a partner to spar with," Hades admits. "But which of you will have that honor?"

"Don't look at me. I just got dragged into this," Giganta says and points to the golden lasso around her ankle.

"I don't want that honor, either," Wonder Woman says. Hades ignores her.

"Then the two of you will do battle to see which is a more worthy opponent," Hades says.

"What if we refuse?" Wonder Woman asks.

Hades snaps his fingers and a giant Minotaur suddenly appears. The creature has the upper body of a man and the lower body of a bull. It immediately charges toward Wonder Woman and Giganta.

"You will either battle each other or you will battle my Minotaur. You have no choice," Hades replies.

"There's always a choice," Wonder Woman says and runs forward toward the Minotaur. Giganta is still tied to the golden lasso and is forced to follow.

But Wonder Woman does not attack the monster. She runs with Amazon speed toward the River Styx that flows past the palace of Hades. Wonder Woman snaps the lasso holding Giganta, and the villain goes flying toward the rushing river.

"Nooo!" Hades yells.

SPLAAAASH! The women land in the river and start to swim.

If Wonder Woman swims into the pit of Tartarus, turn to page 12.

If Wonder Woman guides them to the Elysian Fields, turn to page 14.

If Wonder Woman takes them to the Fields of Asphodel, turn to page 16.

Wonder Woman and Giganta splash into the dark waters of the River Styx. Its strong current carries them away from Hades. They have escaped his plans for them, but now the river has become their enemy. Giganta grows in size to increase her strength and stay above water. Wonder Woman struggles to swim next to her, determined to keep the villain close.

"Where's the shore?" Giganta asks.

"I can't see it," Wonder Woman replies. "Just keep swimming."

There is no sunlight in the Underworld. Wonder Woman and Giganta can't see very far. But they soon hear the roaring sound of a waterfall. The noise gets closer and closer. Wonder Woman grabs onto Giganta.

"Hold on! We're going over!" the hero shouts.

Wonder Woman and Giganta tumble over the top of the waterfall and fall through the dark gloom. Before the hero can use her power of flight to slow them down, they land in the waters of a lake.

Disturbed by their sudden arrival, something huge rises from the water. The head and upper body of a giant man emerges. His lower body, made of serpents, follows.

"Who has fallen into the Pit of Tartarus?" he says. He scoops up Wonder Woman and Giganta and holds them in his palm.

"Who we are is not important," Wonder Woman says. "But I recognize you—Typhon of the first gods, the Titans."

Held high in Typhon's hand, Wonder Woman looks around for the shore. She can barely see in the gray gloom. It is very far away. She has to decide if she and Giganta should try to escape or try to make peace with Typhon.

If Wonder Woman and Giganta try to escape, turn to page 18.

If Wonder Woman decides to make peace with Typhon, turn to page 25.

Wonder Woman and Giganta swim in the River Styx. It is the river that the ferryman, Charon, uses to carry the dead from the land of the living to the realms of Hades's kingdom. The rough current tosses Wonder Woman and Giganta as it carries them swiftly downstream. Wonder Woman uses the river to take them away from Hades and Cerberus.

Soon Wonder Woman sees a shoreline. She swims toward it, pulling Giganta behind her. Wonder Woman releases Giganta from the lasso, and they climb onto dry land. When they step ashore, they see gentle, rolling hills of golden grass with groves of oak and apple trees bathed in gentle sunlight.

"We must be in Elysium, the land of the blessed and honored dead," the hero says.

"Is that a centaur?" Giganta asks and points to a figure under a tree nearby.

"Yes," Wonder Woman says. "He might know a way out of the Underworld."

When they approach, the centaur greets them warmly. It is Chiron, the scholar. But even with all his knowledge, he does not know the way out of Hades's realm.

"But you could ask Orpheus. He left the Underworld once," Chiron says. He points to a building on a nearby hill. "That's his palace."

Wonder Woman and Giganta start to walk toward the hill. Suddenly Wonder Woman hears the sounds of battle. She spots Amazons fighting armored warriors in the distance!

"I wonder what they're fighting about," Wonder Woman says.

"Who cares? Let's go talk to Orpheus," Giganta replies.

If Wonder Woman goes to see what the fight is about, turn to page 20.

If Wonder Woman continues to Orpheus's palace, turn to page 27.

Wonder Woman and Giganta swim along with the current as best they can. It carries them swiftly away from Hades and deep into the dark gloom of the Underworld. They cannot see the shore. The golden lasso is still around Giganta's ankle. Wonder Woman holds onto it so that she and Giganta will not get separated. Suddenly Giganta cries out in alarm.

"Hey! Something just brushed up against my leg!" Giganta says.

"I just felt it too. I think it's the same something," Wonder Woman says.

The head of a giant serpent emerges from the water and stares at them. Then it lunges at the Amazon warrior.

Wonder Woman dodges the river monster, and it bites the golden lasso instead. The lasso is pulled from her hand, but the monster can't hold onto the slim rope and drops it. Giganta is no longer tethered to Wonder Woman, so the villain swims away from the creature and Wonder Woman as fast as she can.

Wonder Woman looks around for Giganta. She can't spot her, but she sees someone else not too far away. It is a ragged old man steering a raft. Wonder Woman recognizes him instantly.

"That's Charon," Wonder Woman says. "He's the ferryman of the dead."

Wonder Woman ponders if she should reach out to the ferryman for help or keep searching for Giganta.

If Wonder Woman swims to Charon, turn to page 23.
If Wonder Woman spots Giganta, turn to page 29.

"Giganta, the lake shore is way over there. Wait for my signal to make a break for it," Wonder Woman says. She points to the water's edge in the distance.

"Why wait?" Giganta says. She suddenly grows to enormous size and leaps from Typhon's palm.

"What?!" Typhon exclaims in surprise.

Wonder Woman dives into the water right behind Giganta. The women swim as fast as they can. They are not fast enough. Up from the murky lake rises another tremendous Titan. It is Echidna, the half-woman, half-serpent wife of Typhon. Snakes grow from her head instead of hair. She reaches out for Giganta.

Wonder Woman unties her lasso from Giganta and uses it to snag Echidna's wrist. The hero pulls back the Titan's hand and keeps her from grabbing Giganta. Suddenly Wonder Woman is grabbed from behind. Typhon's serpent half wraps around the Amazon and lifts her out of the water.

"You are impressive," Typhon says.

"I am Diana of Themyscira, daughter of Queen Hippolyta," Wonder Woman replies. She snaps her golden lasso like a whip, tossing Echidna into Typhon. The two Titans clash and tumble into the water.

Wonder Woman detaches her lasso and launches into the air. She spots Giganta swimming for shore. The Amazon swoops down and plucks Giganta from the lake. Then she flies toward the shore. But she has to decide what to do once they get there.

If Wonder Woman keeps on flying, turn to page 32.
If Wonder Woman decides to land, turn to page 49.

"I want to see what's going on with those Amazons," Wonder Woman decides. "Orpheus can wait for a little while."

"Not me," Giganta says. "I'm getting out of here as soon as I can. You're on your own." She grows ten feet tall and walks away on giant legs.

Wonder Woman heads toward the battle. As she gets near, she is excited to recognize many famous Amazons from history.

"There are Penthesilea and Antiope! Oh, and Marpesia and Orithia too!" the hero gasps.

Then Wonder Woman sees Penthesilea's opponent. It is the warrior Achilles! In life they fought each other in the Trojan War. They are still at it in death. Wonder Woman decides to help her sister Amazon. She leaps into the battle against Achilles.

Achilles is surprised at the sight of this strange Amazon. Wonder Woman uses his moment of distraction to block his sword blow with one of her silver bracelets. *CLANG!*

Turn to page 22.

The impact knocks Achilles off his feet. He lands on his back and starts to laugh!

"Magnificent! This is the first time I've been beaten!" Achilles says.

Penthesilea helps him to his feet as the other warriors surround them. They all want to know who the new Amazon is.

"I am Diana, daughter of Hippolyta," Wonder Woman says. "Hades took me from the Upper World to be his sparring partner, but I escaped."

"An Amazon does not bend to the will of a man, even a god," Antiope says.

"I need to get back home. Do you know a way out of the Underworld?" Wonder Woman asks.

They tell her about a cave. Wonder Woman goes to find Giganta to tell her the good news, but finds her running across the meadow.

"I can't believe it," Wonder Woman says. "She's leaving me behind!"

If Wonder Woman goes after Giganta, turn to page 34.
If Wonder Woman lets Giganta find her own way, turn to page 52.

Wonder Woman decides to swim toward Charon. She hopes he will help her find Giganta. The ferryman is surprised to see Wonder Woman when she grips the edge of his raft.

"What?! Who goes there?" Charon asks.

"A wayward traveler. Permission to come aboard?" Wonder Woman asks.

"How unusual!" Charon says. "And what a pleasant change from my dreary routine. Permission granted."

Charon helps Wonder Woman out of the water. When he touches her warm, living hand, he is even more surprised.

"You are not dead!" Charon says.

"Hades kidnapped me and . . . um . . . my friend from the Upper World," Wonder Woman explains. "The River Styx carried her away. Will you help me find her?"

Charon peers downstream through the gloom. His eyes are adapted to the darkness. He points to a figure in the water in the distance.

Turn the page.

"I see your friend," Charon says. He guides his ferry toward Giganta.

When Giganta sees Wonder Woman she starts to swim away, trying to escape the super hero. Wonder Woman reaches down and grabs the loose end of the golden lasso trailing in the water. The other end is still tied to Giganta's ankle. Wonder Woman pulls Giganta toward the ferry and onto the deck.

Charon steers the raft down the river to a dock. There is a small house on the shore. Wonder Woman and Giganta step onto the dock as Charon ties up the raft.

"Would you like to come into my home?" Charon asks. "I seldom have visitors."

Wonder Woman and Giganta must decide whether to accept his invitation or not.

If Wonder Woman and Giganta accept his offer, turn to page 36.

If Wonder Woman and Giganta go on their way, turn to page 55.

Wonder Woman decides to try and make peace with the ancient god. She unties her lasso from Giganta and hooks it to her belt as a sign of surrender.

"Oh great Typhon! We give up! Be merciful to us!" Wonder Woman says and kneels in the palm of the giant's hand.

"What?" Giganta gasps in surprise.

"Shhh! Just do as I do, and we might get out of this alive," Wonder Woman whispers. Giganta kneels but frowns at Wonder Woman.

"Who asks mercy of Typhon?" the Titan asks.

"I am Princess Diana of Themyscira, daughter of Hippolyta, Queen of the Amazons," Wonder Woman says. She nudges Giganta in the arm with her elbow.

"Oh! I'm called Giganta—for obvious reasons," Giganta says, growing thirty feet tall.

Typhon laughs. Giganta's talent amuses him.

Turn the page.

"Merciful Typhon, we are mortals and do not belong here. Will you tell us the way to the Upper World?" Wonder Woman asks. "We will tell the glorious tale of meeting you to all of the world!"

"Spreading it thick much?" Giganta mutters.

"The path is dangerous for mortals, but if you succeed it will be a thrilling part of your tale!" Typhon says.

* * *

Soon the hero and villain walk across the empty landscape, following Typhon's directions.

"All I see are rocks. What's so dangerous about rocks?" Giganta says.

Suddenly they hear a screeching from above. Huge birds flap toward them shooting metal feathers! The only shelter is a pair of boulders. But a dragon sleeps between them.

"Now what?" Giganta asks.

If Wonder Woman and Giganta battle the birds, turn to page 68.

If Wonder Woman and Giganta face the dragon, turn to page 87.

Wonder Woman decides it is more important to talk to Orpheus about a way out of the Underworld. She puts aside her curiosity about the Amazons battling in the distance.

When Wonder Woman and Giganta arrive at the palace of Orpheus, they discover that it looks like a Greek temple with stone columns holding up the roof. Inside it is filled with riches that make Giganta's eyes go wide.

"Is everyone rich in Elysium?" Giganta asks.

"Elysium is whatever the dead want it to be. It is their heaven," Wonder Woman says.

They hear music and follow it to the center of the palace. There they find Orpheus, the greatest musician in Greek myth. He plays on a golden harp called a lyre.

The music is so beautiful that Wonder Woman and Giganta cannot resist listening to it. They can hardly focus on anything else. They came to the palace for a reason, but now they can't remember why. Wonder Woman realizes they are in danger!

Turn the page.

It takes Wonder Woman's intense willpower to break free. She reaches out and grabs the lyre from Orpheus. The music stops.

"Don't you like my music?" Orpheus asks.

"Too much," Wonder Woman says. "But we came to ask for directions, not for a song."

Wonder Woman asks Orpheus where he escaped the Underworld. The myth is famous, but the location of the exit is not. Orpheus tells them about a cave not far away. Wonder Woman and Giganta leave the palace and head across the meadow. In the distance, they see a band of centaurs.

If Wonder Woman and Giganta head toward the centaurs, turn to page 72.

If Wonder Woman and Giganta avoid the centaurs, turn to page 89.

Wonder Woman spots Giganta climbing onto dry land not far away and swims toward her. Giganta walks swiftly inland. She either does not see Wonder Woman or is trying to escape from her. The super-villain still has the golden lasso around her ankle and drags it after her.

Wonder Woman climbs out of the river and follows Giganta across a vast field of tall white flowers. They have a unique shape that Wonder Woman recognizes.

"These are asphodel flowers. I must be in the part of the Underworld known as the Fields of Asphodel," Wonder Woman says. "This is not a good place to be. I better catch up to Giganta quickly."

Wonder Woman uses her Amazon strength to leap across the meadow and land next to Giganta. But before Wonder Woman can pick up the end of the lasso, ghostly shapes suddenly surround them. The ghosts are solid and grab Wonder Woman and Giganta.

Turn the page.

"Ow! These guys are ice cold!" Giganta says.

"These are the ghosts of the vengeful dead," Wonder Woman says, shaking off the ghost that grabbed her. "They were murderers, thieves, and criminals once, and they are still evil."

"Well don't just stand there," Giganta says. "Do something!"

Wonder Woman grabs the end of her lasso and unfastens it from Giganta's ankle. Then she throws it around the threatening ghosts and twirls them above her head.

WHOOSH! WHOOSH! WHOOSH!

Wonder Woman releases the lasso and the ghouls sail far across the meadow. But more ghosts close in and surround them instantly.

"Nice try, Princess," Giganta says. "But they've got us outnumbered! What are we going to do?"

"We have to get out of here," Wonder Woman says. "We can either retreat or go forward."

If Wonder Woman and Giganta dive back into the Styx, turn to page 74.

If Wonder Woman and Giganta fight their way past the ghouls, turn to page 93.

Wonder Woman decides it is safer to keep flying. She has no way of knowing what other dangers lurk below. Tartarus is a terrible place of monsters and punishment.

Suddenly Wonder Woman and Giganta hear an ear-splitting screech. It comes from a creature flying straight toward them. The beast has the head and wings of an eagle and a lion's body.

"A griffin! The sky isn't safe either," Wonder Woman says.

"Some rescue," Giganta grumbles.

The griffin beats its giant wings and speeds toward Wonder Woman and Giganta. It snaps its beak in warning.

"I don't want to fight you," Wonder Woman says. She dodges the griffin's charge.

Giganta shrinks to normal human size so that she can hold on as Wonder Woman zigzags through the air trying to avoid the flying beast. But the griffin chases them like a bird of prey. It matches every turn Wonder Woman makes.

"Ooooh, I'm getting dizzy," Giganta groans.

Wonder Woman swoops and turns. She dives toward the ground and then soars into the gray skies. The griffin is a creature of myth and has the same amazing speed of the Amazon Princess. It strikes out at Wonder Woman with lion claws and tries to catch her in its sharp beak.

"This tactic isn't working. I have to find another way to deal with this beast," Wonder Woman says.

"Just hurry up, or I'm going to be sick," Giganta moans.

Turn to page 38.

Wonder Woman chases after Giganta. It is still her duty to bring the villain to justice in the Upper World. The hero uses her Amazon strength to make a huge leap toward Giganta.

THOMP!

Wonder Woman lands in front of the villain.

"Going somewhere without me?" Wonder Woman says.

"Yes! Orpheus told me where to find the exit," Giganta says. "I told you before you were on your own."

Giganta grows fifteen feet tall and steps over Wonder Woman. The Amazon tosses her golden lasso. It wraps around Giganta and tightens around her torso and arms.

"Stop," Wonder Woman commands. Giganta stops. "Return to normal size."

Giganta shrinks back down to human size. The lasso stays tight around her. Wonder Woman leads Giganta across the meadow.

Wonder Woman and Giganta have not gone far before they see a large herd of deer charging toward them at tremendous speed. A huge plume of dust rises up behind them.

"It's a stampede!" Wonder Woman says.

Wonder Woman tells Giganta to stand behind her. Then the hero plants her feet to steady herself. She uses her remarkable Amazon strength to clap her metal bracelets together. A thunderous shock wave of sound erupts.

BOOOOM!

The sound hits the herd, disrupting their wild charge. They scatter before they reach Wonder Woman and Giganta.

"I wonder what made those animals stampede like that," Wonder Woman says. Then she sees a giant man running after the herd of deer.

Turn to page 42.

Wonder Woman decides to accept Charon's invitation. She starts to follow the ferryman to his house, but Giganta lags behind.

"Why are we wasting time with that old guy?" Giganta complains. "We should be looking for a way out of here."

"Because Charon ferries the dead across the Styx to the realms of the Underworld. The dead come from the Upper World through a portal. I bet he knows where it is," Wonder Woman says.

"Oh," Giganta says.

Wonder Woman removes her golden lasso from Giganta's ankle, and they follow Charon through the door of the small house.

"Oh my!" Giganta exclaims.

The interior of the small house is actually a huge palace. The entrance hall is a vast room filled with hundreds of treasures. Statues made of solid gold stand in front of tapestries spun from silver and platinum thread. The floor is a mosaic made of precious stones and gems.

"He's rich!" Giganta says in awe.

"The dead must pay me for their passage to the Underworld. I have collected a lot of coins over many thousands of years," Charon says as he takes off his ragged cloak. It reveals a handsome young man.

Giganta looks even more surprised at his appearance.

"These are just my work clothes," Charon explains. "Let me give you a tour of my home."

Turn to page 45.

Wonder Woman grabs her golden lasso attached to her belt. She twirls it with one hand and tosses it toward the threatening griffin. The creature dodges it.

"You are as swift as Hermes," Wonder Woman tells the beast. "But so am I."

Wonder Woman's arm moves in a blur of motion as she throws the lasso again. It falls over the griffin's head and snares the creature around its neck.

"I command you to stop attacking us," Wonder Woman says.

The griffin halts its attack instantly. It flaps its wings to hover in midair. Wonder Woman flies over to the beast with Giganta, and they sit on the creature's back.

"How did you do that?" Giganta says in surprise.

"The Lasso of Truth makes whoever—or whatever—is held by it obey me," Wonder Woman explains.

Turn to page 40.

"Then tell this creature to get us out of here," Giganta says.

Wonder Woman pats the griffin on the neck like a tame horse. It shakes its head and ruffles its feathers. Then it chirps like a parakeet.

"Good boy. Now, please take us to the Upper World," Wonder Woman says.

The griffin flaps its mighty wings and begins to fly. It soars in one direction, but then it turns around and flies back the way it came. It tries flying in another direction, but then it seems confused. Finally the griffin ends up circling above the barren landscape, going nowhere.

"It doesn't know how to get to the Upper World," Wonder Woman says.

"Oh great. Now what are we going to do?" Giganta says.

Wonder Woman tells the griffin to land. She and Giganta slide off the beast's back. Wonder Woman gives the griffin one last command.

"Go away, and do not attack us again," Wonder Woman says.

Wonder Woman releases the creature from the golden lasso. The beast flaps its giant wings and takes off into the sky. It flies away from Wonder Woman and Giganta and does not look back.

"I suppose it's up to us to find our own way out of the Underworld," Wonder Woman says.

"You and I are always on opposite sides. But this time I'm with you all the way," Giganta says. "There's no way I'm staying here to be Hades's sparring partner."

Wonder Woman and Giganta walk together across the barren land in search of a way home.

THE END

To follow another path, turn to page 11.

The man chasing the deer is ten feet tall and carries a giant bronze club. He wears an animal pelt for clothing, and the belt around his waist has three large gemstones. He stops when he sees Wonder Woman and Giganta.

"Help! I'm being held prisoner by this savage Amazon!" Giganta tells the giant. "Free me and I will reward you!"

"What?! You are not a prisoner," Wonder Woman says.

The giant looks at the lasso binding Giganta.

"This lasso just keeps her from running away," Wonder Woman explains. "I've had to chase her down once already."

"I was trying to escape my cruel captor!" Giganta says.

"Release her," the giant tells Wonder Woman.

"Okay, but it's your fault if she gets away," Wonder Woman says. She releases Giganta from the golden lasso. Giganta immediately grows to twenty feet tall and starts running.

"She is fast. I like it when they are fast," the giant man says and starts running after Giganta.

Wonder Woman flies into the air to watch from above. She knows who the man is and that he will not harm Giganta, but Wonder Woman still wants to make sure Giganta is safe during this little adventure.

The giant is as swift as Giganta and catches up to her quickly. He grabs for her arm, but Giganta evades his grasp. She increases her size and speed on extra-long legs. She is surprised to hear the man laugh with delight.

Giganta cannot escape the giant. She runs in zigzags. She races through groves of trees. She twists and turns and dodges. And still the man follows relentlessly. At last Giganta simply gets tired and stops. She shrinks down to human size and falls to the ground. The man catches up to her and puts his hand on her shoulder.

"Thank you for the wonderful chase!" he says. Then he walks away.

Turn the page.

Wonder Woman lands and ties the golden lasso around Giganta's wrist. When Giganta catches her breath again, she asks Wonder Woman who the man was.

"That was Orion the Hunter of myth," Wonder Woman says. "He loves the chase, and you gave him one of the best."

Then Wonder Woman leads a weary Giganta across the meadows of Elysium toward the cave to the Upper World that Achilles told her about.

THE END

To follow another path, turn to page 11.

Wonder Woman and Giganta follow Charon through some of the rooms of his palace. Each room is stuffed with treasures. He even has a zoo that contains extinct animals, long dead in the Upper World. Wonder Woman pauses to pet a Triceratops, then she realizes that Giganta has suddenly gone missing.

"Giddy-up!" Giganta yells.

Wonder Woman turns to see Giganta on the back of a huge Spinosaurus. The villain is now twenty feet tall and has a large tapestry of spun silver slung over her back like a sack. It is nearly bursting with Charon's treasures. The Spinosaurus breaks out of its cage and crashes out of the zoo.

"Your companion dares to steal from me!" Charon exclaims.

"I'm sorry, Charon. That's very rude of her," Wonder Woman says. She takes off after the fleeing villain.

Wonder Woman twirls her golden lasso as she runs after Giganta riding the dinosaur.

Turn the page.

"Giganta! Where do you think you're going with that treasure?" Wonder Woman says. "You don't know the way out of the Underworld!"

"I'll find my own way!" Giganta replies. "And I will be rich beyond imagination!"

Wonder Woman throws the golden lasso and snags the sack Giganta carries. She pulls it from Giganta's grip.

"Hey!" Giganta yells. She turns the enormous Spinosaurus around and charges toward the Amazon warrior.

Wonder Woman stands firm in the face of the rushing beast. Then she leaps forward and grabs its leg. With a mighty heave, Wonder Woman lifts the dinosaur and slams it to the ground. The creature is stunned senseless. So is Giganta.

Charon arrives and takes the sack of treasure.

"Thank you for recovering my belongings," Charon says to Wonder Woman. "I know you seek the way out of the Underworld and I will tell you its location. But this thief will stay."

Turn to page 48.

"But I can't just leave her behind," Wonder Woman says.

"Fear not. I promise to send her to the Upper World," Charon says. "After she repairs the damage to my zoo and cleans all the cages."

"That sounds like a fair sentence," Wonder Woman says.

"You do not know how large my zoo is," Charon says with a knowing smile.

THE END

To follow another path, turn to page 11.

Wonder Woman carries Giganta to the lakeshore and lands. Not far away stands a large building. It is surrounded by a wall made of tall logs sharpened to points at the tips. A single large gate is the only entrance. A column of smoke rises up from inside the wooden walls.

"It looks like someone is living over there," Wonder Woman says.

"Maybe they know a way out of here!" Giganta exclaims and starts to run toward the building on ten-foot-long legs.

"Wait! We should be careful! Tartarus is home to the most dangerous monsters and beings," Wonder Woman warns, but Giganta ignores her.

Giganta takes giant strides and arrives at the gate in a matter of moments. Wonder Woman catches up to her just as Giganta starts to pound on the gate with her massive fist.

BOOOOM! BOOOOM! BOOOOM!

Turn the page.

"Hey! You in there!" Giganta shouts. "Open up or I'll break down the door!"

"You have no manners," Wonder Woman says quietly and shakes her head.

Suddenly the gate opens. A giant man dressed in armor stands before Wonder Woman and Giganta. He holds a sword in one hand and a shield in the other. But the most impressive thing about him is the single round eye in the middle of his forehead.

"Uh-oh. Cyclops," Wonder Woman says.

"Hi, big guy. We're looking for a way out of the Underworld. Can you give us directions?" Giganta says. She stands as tall as the Cyclops and looks him in the eye.

The giant warrior frowns at Giganta.

"Why should I? You rudely beat on our gate and disturbed our practice. Go away," the Cyclops says.

The Cyclops starts to shut the gate, but Giganta stops it with one enormous foot.

"Then I'll just have to bash the information out of you," Giganta declares and knocks the Cyclops back from the gate.

"Giganta! Don't!" Wonder Woman says.

But it is too late. Giganta and the Cyclops tumble through the gate. It opens wide and Wonder Woman does not like what she sees on the other side!

Turn to page 58.

Wonder Woman watches Giganta run across the fields of Elysium, away from the palace of Orpheus.

"It looks like Orpheus told Giganta where to find the exit to the Upper World. It figures that she would keep that information to herself," Wonder Woman says. "Well, that makes me think she wants to abandon me here in the Underworld."

Wonder Woman sees Giganta disappear into a grove of trees.

"Yes, now I'm sure of it," Wonder Woman says. "Well, Giganta can go her own way. I just happen have my own way out. According to Achilles, a cave near here will get me home."

The Amazon Princess begins her journey across the golden Elysian meadows. A gentle breeze ruffles her hair. Warm sunlight touches her skin. This part of the Underworld feels completely different than the dark gloom of the other regions of Hades's realm.

The Elysian meadows are where the heroes of myth dwell in eternal happiness. Warriors like Achilles and Penthesilea enjoy everlasting battle. Scholars like Chiron spend eternity reading and studying. It is a realm without care or worry or fear. That is why Wonder Woman is very surprised when she hears a cry for help!

Wonder Woman follows the cry to a thick grove of apple trees. The cries come from inside the grove. Wonder Woman enters the grove and works her way to the center. There, she sees Giganta!

"Help! I'm trapped!" Giganta moans.

Giganta is up in the branches of a large apple tree. The tree limbs are curved around her like the bars of a cage. Wonder Woman sees Giganta holding a fistful of golden apples and realizes the reason for Giganta's situation.

"Giganta! You were trying to steal the Golden Apples of the Hesperides," Wonder Woman says. "And the dryads who protect them caught you."

Turn the page.

Giganta tries to grow in size and burst through the branches, but they hold tight. The limbs squeeze the villain, forcing her to reduce her size.

"Give up the apples," Wonder Woman says.

"No," Giganta says stubbornly.

"If you let go of the apples, the dryads will let go of you," Wonder Woman says.

Suddenly the leaves and branches of the nearby trees sway and rustle. The bark on the tree trunks shifts. Female faces form. Wonder Woman sees that their expressions are not happy.

Turn to page 62.

Wonder Woman decides it would be a good idea to leave the Underworld as soon as possible.

"Thank you for your invitation, Charon, but we can't stay," Wonder Woman says. "We must find a way out of the Underworld before Hades catches up to us."

"I know of only one way out of the Underworld, and that is the way in," Charon says. He points up the river, back toward Hades's palace. "The dead enter Hades's realm through a portal on the banks of the Styx. You may leave the Underworld through that portal, but you must cross the river to reach it."

"Can't you ferry us over there?" Giganta asks.

"I ferry the dead," Charon says. "Ferrying the living is not in my job description."

Wonder Woman and Giganta leave Charon and walk along the shore. The landscape looks barren and gloomy. A few dead trees stand like dry bones in the hard, rocky soil. There is no sun. There are no clouds. The only light comes from the glow of the golden lasso.

Turn the page.

"Will you take that lasso off my ankle?" Giganta asks. "I'm not going to run away. There's nowhere to go."

"All right. We are in this together," Wonder Woman says and unties the lasso.

Suddenly Wonder Woman sees something through the gloom. Hades rides toward them on the back of a skeleton horse. Its black bones gleam in the dim light and its sharp hooves strike sparks on the rocky ground. Cerberus runs beside the horse like a hound on the hunt. He howls as soon as he catches their living scent.

Giganta turns and starts to flee.

"You said you weren't going to run away!" Wonder Woman says.

"You didn't compel me to tell the truth!" Giganta replies.

"But we can fight Hades together as a team!" Wonder Woman says.

"No way! It's every girl for herself!" Giganta says. She grows to enormous size and runs across the barren landscape on twenty-foot-long legs.

Wonder Woman stands her ground and prepares to meet Hades head-on. Cerberus bounds past her and chases after Giganta. Hades pulls his mount to a stop in front of Wonder Woman.

"You are full of surprises," Hades says.

Turn to page 65.

Wonder Woman sees a group of at least twenty Cyclops soldiers inside the wooden walls. They are practicing against each other with their swords and shields. They stop when they see Giganta and the Cyclops roll through the gate. Wonder Woman looks at their armor and realizes who they are.

"These are the Cyclops warriors who helped Zeus defeat the Titans and win Olympus. But then Zeus banished them to Tartarus," Wonder Woman says. "They are famous even in the Upper World."

"Never heard of them," Giganta says. She shakes her fist in the face of the Cyclops she has knocked down. "Now, are you going to tell me the way out of here, or what?"

Suddenly the rest of the giant soldiers surround her.

"I will tell you only if you defeat me in battle," says the Cyclops sprawled on the ground at Giganta's feet.

"Okay," Giganta says and grows to an even larger size. She looms over the Cyclops and his comrades.

Suddenly all twenty Cyclops soldiers swarm Giganta. They climb up her legs like tree trunks. Their weight makes Giganta lose her balance.

"Hey, that's cheating!" Giganta says. "I could use a little help here, Princess!"

Wonder Woman leaps to Giganta's aid. She uses her Amazon strength to pry a few soldiers from Giganta and toss them across the practice field. Giganta regains her balance and shakes off the Cyclops warriors gripping her. They run toward Wonder Woman with swords raised.

CLAAANG!

Wonder Woman blocks their blades with her bracelets. *CRAAACK!* The swords shatter.

Then Wonder Woman raises her arms and claps her bracelets together.

BOOOM!

Turn to page 61.

The shock wave knocks out the Cyclops soldiers. Wonder Woman looks up at Giganta.

"You can take it from here," the hero says.

Giganta dangles her Cyclops challenger by his collar with two fingers.

"Give up?" she asks the Cyclops.

"You win!" the warrior replies. "I'll tell you the way to the Upper World."

Wonder Woman and Giganta soon leave the Cyclops, and his soldiers, behind. They walk across the barren landscape of Tartarus. Giganta looks pleased, but Wonder Woman frowns.

"What's the matter? We won! The Cyclops told us how to get home," Giganta says.

"I hope he told us the truth. He cheated before," Wonder Woman says. "He could be sending us into a trap."

In the distance, they hear a monster roar.

"That cheater," Giganta grumbles.

THE END

To follow another path, turn to page 11.

The female faces do not speak, but they show their annoyance in other ways. The lower branches of the trees swipe at Wonder Woman. It is like having a dozen wooden clubs swinging at her head. Wonder Woman uses her Amazon speed to dodge the blows.

Sapling trees suddenly sprout out of the ground at Wonder Woman's feet. The tender shoots twist around her legs. They grow up her body, trying to encase her. Wonder Woman reaches up and grabs one of the tree branches swiping at her head. She uses the branch to pull herself free of the saplings's snare.

"I mean you no harm!" Wonder Woman says to the tree dryads. "Just let Giganta go and we will leave."

"Here! You can have your stupid apples!" Giganta says, throwing the golden apples to the ground. Her action seems to anger the dryads even more.

"You just insulted them by throwing away the golden apples," Wonder Woman says.

"They get mad if I take the apples and are mad if I toss them. Why don't they make up their minds?!" Giganta grumbles.

"There is only one cure for their anger and that is love," Wonder Woman says.

Wonder Woman dodges past the slashing branches and whipping saplings to the base of the largest apple tree. She wraps her arms around the tree trunk and gives it a warm embrace.

"It never hurts to hug a tree," the hero says.

The tree dryad responds to Wonder Woman's act of love. The branches stop swaying. The leaves go quiet. Wonder Woman goes around to all the trees in the grove and gives each of them a warm hug. At last she embraces the tree dryad holding Giganta captive.

"Now say you're sorry, Giganta," Wonder Woman says.

"Sorry," Giganta says in a quiet voice. The branches open up and release her.

Turn the page.

"Thank you," Wonder Woman tells the tree dryad.

Giganta leaps out of the tree and runs from the grove. She sees Wonder Woman walk out soon after. The Amazon holds a golden apple.

"The dryads are very friendly once you get to know them. And generous too," Wonder Woman says. "Now, let's go home. I know the way."

THE END

To follow another path, turn to page 11.

"Be careful what you wish for," Wonder Woman says as she leaps toward the Lord of the Dead with her fists clenched.

Wonder Woman uses her Amazon bracelets to smash Hades's skeleton horse. It shatters and falls to pieces under him. Hades falls to the ground in a heap. He looks startled.

"Surprise," Wonder Woman says.

Hades smiles and jumps to his feet. His hands glow and form two flaming swords. Hades leaps to attack Wonder Woman. She blocks the fiery weapons with her bracelets. *SIZZZZLE!* Hades uses his Olympian strength to push Wonder Woman backward. Wonder Woman uses her Amazon strength to resist.

"Give up," Hades says.

"Never," Wonder Woman replies.

Wonder Woman strikes her bracelets against the flaming swords. The flames explode with each blow.

BLAM! BLAM! BLAM!

Turn the page.

The dark gloom of the Underworld lights up. Wonder Woman's fierce counter-attack forces Hades backward step by step. Suddenly his back is to the River Styx.

"Give up," Wonder Woman tells Hades.

Suddenly Hades laughs, but it is not in defiance. He surprises Wonder Woman by snuffing out the flaming swords. Then he hugs her!

"Thank you!" Hades says. "You have cured me of my boredom!"

"Um, you're welcome," Wonder Woman replies.

"You fought as well as any of the dead heroes in the Underworld," Hades says. "Better, in fact. Even Achilles could not push me to the brink of the Styx like you did."

"I'm glad you're happy," Wonder Woman says. "Now, can Giganta and I go home?"

"I should keep you here to fight future battles, but I am feeling generous," Hades says. He whistles for Cerberus.

The triple-headed hound bounds across the rocky plain in answer to his master's call. Giganta squirms between one of his jaws.

"Cerberus will take you back to the Upper World," Hades says.

The hound moves to take Wonder Woman into one of its jaws, but she steps back.

"I'll sit on his back, where it's dry," Wonder Woman says.

THE END

To follow another path, turn to page 11.

"The birds are the immediate threat," Wonder Woman decides.

The creatures fire their metal feathers at Wonder Woman and Giganta. Wonder Woman uses her bracelets to deflect the feathers. They are as sharp as daggers. **PING! TINK!**

Giganta grows to enormous size and swipes at the flock of birds as if they are a swarm of mosquitoes. She bats one out of the sky and it lands at Wonder Woman's feet. It has a long, bronze beak.

"Metal feathers and beaks of bronze. I know what these birds are," Wonder Woman says. "They're the Stymphalian Birds of myth. Hercules fought them as his Sixth Labor."

"Stim-fal-what kind of birds?" Giganta says. "Why is everything in Greek mythology so hard to pronounce!"

Giganta smacks more of the birds away from her. They are hurled hundreds of feet away. They fall on the sleeping dragon and poke him with their sharp beaks.

Turn to page 70.

ROAAAR!

The dragon bellows and wakes up.

"Oops," Giganta says.

The giant beast uncurls like a snake and stands up on four short legs. Sharp spikes line the length of its back. Black scales gleam in the dark gloom of the Underworld. Its eyes are as red as burning embers, and they turn in the direction of Wonder Woman and Giganta. The creature starts to lumber toward them.

"Uh, Princess, I think we have a problem," Giganta says.

Wonder Woman hears the dragon bellow. She can feel the thump of its weight shake the ground. But she cannot take her attention away from the attacking birds.

"You can handle it, Giganta," Wonder Woman says. "I believe in you!"

"If you say so," the villain replies. "But don't blame me if you don't like how this turns out."

Giganta watches the dragon charge toward her. She increases her height to the maximum. She is now three times the size of the beast.

"No contest," Giganta says. She stomps her foot down in front of the dragon.

WHOOOOOMP!

Loose rocks and gravel spray into the air from the impact. The dragon stops in surprise. Giganta waves her giant arms at the creature and shouts.

"Shoo! Go away! Beat it!" the villain says. Her voice is almost as loud as the dragon's roar.

Turn to page 76.

Wonder Woman recognizes one of the centaurs in the distance.

"Look, it's Chiron," Wonder Woman says. "He's the one who told us to talk to Orpheus. Let's go thank him for his advice."

"Okay, but let's make it quick. I want to get out of here, even if it is the Greek version of heaven," Giganta says.

As Wonder Woman and Giganta get near, they see that the centaurs are having contests of skill. One group competes in the discus throw, another has an archery contest, and a third group's members race each other across the meadow.

"Hello, Chiron!" Wonder Woman shouts and waves.

The centaur scholar sees them and smiles. He waves for them to come to his side.

"You were right about Orpheus knowing a way out of the Underworld," Wonder Woman says. "But I wish you had warned us about how . . . captivating his music is."

"It has been known to make even grim Hades weep," Chiron admits.

"I see we have two new players for our games!" a centaur says as he gallops up to Chiron. The centaur is a handsome male with long black hair and a shiny brown hide. He smiles extra brightly at Giganta and winks.

"What do I get when I win?" Giganta asks.

"*When* you win? Those are bold words coming from a creature with only two little legs," the centaur replies.

Giganta grows twenty feet tall and lifts the centaur with one hand.

"On second thought, you will be perfect for the weight-lifting contest," the centaur says with a laugh.

Turn to page 79.

"The best way out of here is back the way we came—the River Styx!" Wonder Woman says.

Giganta grows to enormous size and takes giant strides toward the river. Wonder Woman leaps after her. The ghouls race across the flowery field in pursuit.

"I hope these guys can't swim," Giganta says.

SPLAAASHH!

Wonder Woman and Giganta dive into the dark waters of the Styx and let the current carry them away. But they are not out of danger. The head of a giant serpent lifts up out of the water and turns its red eyes toward them.

"A ketos—a sea monster!" the hero says.

"What's a sea monster doing in a river?" Giganta asks.

"This is the Underworld. Anything is possible," Wonder Woman replies.

"Is it the same monster that attacked us before?" Giganta asks.

"I don't think that really matters," Wonder Woman says.

The creature swims toward them and bares its sharp fangs. **ROAAAR!**

Giganta grows to a stupendous size and gets ready to deliver a giant punch to the huge creature. But Wonder Woman twirls her lasso and tosses it around the serpent's neck. The golden lasso glows.

"Be calm," Wonder Woman commands the angry beast.

The monster stops its attack and grows tame. Wonder Woman climbs onto its back. Giganta does the same.

"You will carry us to safety," Wonder Woman instructs the ketos. It starts to swim down the River Styx.

"That golden lasso sure comes in handy," Giganta says.

"It is a more peaceful way to handle a threat," Wonder Woman says.

Turn to page 83.

The dragon sees the gigantic human in front of it and decides against attacking. It turns and thumps away from Giganta.

"That was easier than I thought," Giganta says.

She watches to make sure the dragon is gone. Then she returns to normal human size and turns to see what is happening with Wonder Woman. The Amazon Princess stands in the middle of a circle of metal feathers. The Stymphalian Birds have shot all their feathers at the Amazon until they have none left. The birds wander on the ground nearby, flightless. They look like plucked turkeys.

"They're not so dangerous now," Giganta says.

"They're just tired. Let's leave before they recover," Wonder Woman says.

Wonder Woman and Giganta continue their journey following the directions Typhon gave them. They walk across the empty plain of rocks and gravel.

With no large landmarks to guide them, Giganta worries that they will get lost and wander forever. But at last Wonder Woman's sharp sight spots a lone hill in the distance. On top of the hill is a stone arch.

"That must be the exit!" Giganta says.

Giganta grows to her fullest height and runs on giant legs toward the gate. Wonder Woman uses her Amazon strength to leap after Giganta. They arrive at the gate at the same time. There is someone waiting there for them.

Wonder Woman and Giganta face a young man with wings. He holds a sword in one hand and stands in front of the gate.

"I am Thanatos, Guardian of the Gate. No one may leave the Underworld," he says.

"It seems that Typhon gave us directions to the exit from the Underworld but didn't tell us it was guarded," Wonder Woman says. "It looks like we are going to have to fight our way out of here."

Turn the page.

"Wait. Cousin Typhon told you about the gate?" Thanatos asks. "In that case you may pass. But he's really not supposed to do that. I'm going to have to scold him about revealing the gate's secret at the next family gathering."

Thanatos opens the gate and stands aside. Wonder Woman and Giganta step through. Suddenly they are in the Upper World. Giganta holds out her wrists to Wonder Woman.

"What are you doing?" Wonder Woman asks in surprise.

"I want you to tie me up and take me to prison where it's *safe!*" Giganta says.

THE END

To follow another path, turn to page 11.

As Giganta thumps over to the centaurs lifting boulders as feats of strength, Wonder Woman decides to test her archery skills. She joins the line of centaur archers and lifts one of the giant bows. The centaurs stop to watch her pull back a large arrow and aim at the distant target.

THWAAANG!

The arrow flies like a missile and pierces the center of the bull's-eye.

THUNK!

"A perfect shot!" the centaurs shout. Their cheering gets the attention of the centaurs throwing javelins. They want Wonder Woman to compete with them too.

Wonder Woman lifts one of the long, thin javelins to feel its weight and balance. She sights down the field to where the other javelin throws have landed. Wonder Woman takes a few running steps and launches the slender rod down the field.

WHOOSH!

Turn the page.

Wonder Woman's javelin sails far beyond the others and lands hundreds of feet down the field.

THUNK!

The centaurs cheer wildly and gather around her. One of them lifts her onto his back and starts to gallop. The other centaurs quickly follow. They race across the fields of Elysium toward the weight-lifting competition.

The laughing and yelling centaurs gallop around Giganta's legs. Wonder Woman rides on the back of the centaur with the natural skill of an Amazon on a horse. Giganta hops from one foot to the other to avoid stepping on the playful centaurs. She holds a centaur in each hand and tries not to drop them as she bounces from foot to foot. But they only laugh at the antics of their friends on the ground.

"Feast! Feast! A feast for our new champions!" the centaurs shout.

"I guess we can stay for dinner," Wonder Woman says.

Turn to page 82.

It does not take long for the centaurs to bring out food and drinks. Lyre music starts to play and singing begins. The tune is not as captivating as Orpheus's music, but the centaurs raise their voices in song. Wonder Woman is surprised to hear them sing about her and Giganta.

The music continues as the centaurs walk with Wonder Woman and Giganta to Orpheus's cave—the exit from the Underworld. It was not very far after all.

Wonder Woman and Giganta wave goodbye and enter the cave. They climb up the dark tunnel toward home as the music of the centaurs fades behind them.

THE END

To follow another path, turn to page 11.

The ketos monster carries Wonder Woman and Giganta down the River Styx. They soon come to a place where another river merges with the Styx. It is a river of fire!

"The Phlegethon!" Wonder Woman says.

"The fleg-a-what? How do you know these things?" Giganta asks.

"To you this is mythology. To me it's history," Wonder Woman replies.

The ketos monster refuses to go near the flaming river. Wonder Woman doesn't blame the beast. She guides it to the riverbank of the Styx. Wonder Woman and Giganta jump onto dry land.

"Come on," Wonder Woman says. "We must walk from here,"

"To where?" Giganta asks.

"To where Odysseus once entered the Underworld. I read about it in *The Odyssey*. You should read it sometime," Wonder Woman says.

"Sounds boring," Giganta grumbles.

Turn the page.

"Maybe, but it tells me how to get out of here," Wonder Woman says.

Wonder Woman and Giganta trek across a flat, barren landscape covered with small rocks. No plants grow there. It is empty and dead.

"Talk about boring," Giganta says. Then she sees something in the distance. "Or, maybe not. What's that?"

Wonder Woman looks toward where Giganta points. She sees a man pushing a large boulder up the side of a hill.

"It's Sisyphus," Wonder Woman says.

"Hey, even I know who that is," Giganta says. "He's doomed to push a rock up a hill, then have it roll back down. Forever."

"It is his eternal punishment for his evil deeds," Wonder Woman says.

"He needs a break," Giganta says as she runs over to the hill. She grabs the boulder and throws it far away.

"Giganta! No!" Wonder Woman cries.

Turn to page 86.

"There you go, pal," Giganta tells Sisyphus.

Suddenly the boulder turns around in midair. It slams down at the base of the hill.

WHAAAAM! Sisyphus sighs and walks down the hill to start his task again.

"Zeus put a spell on the boulder so that it always returns to the bottom of the hill," Wonder Woman says. "But now he might punish *you* for getting involved."

"What? Let's get out of here!" Giganta says, running downhill past Sisyphus. "Sorry, buddy."

Wonder Woman leads Giganta across the barren plain to a distant grove of trees.

"This is Persephone's Grove, where Odysseus entered the Underworld," Wonder Woman says. "According to *The Odyssey*, the mortal world lies on the other side."

"I think I'm going to read that book," Giganta says as she and Wonder Woman enter the grove.

THE END

To follow another path, turn to page 11.

The metal feathers the strange birds shoot at Wonder Woman and Giganta are as sharp as daggers.

"Let's get to the shelter of those boulders," Wonder Woman decides. "I have an idea about how to deal with the dragon."

Wonder Woman and Giganta run across the barren field of rocks and stones. The metal missiles rain down around them.

ZIIP! ZIIIP!

The birds screech angrily because they keep missing their targets. But the noise disturbs the dragon's sleep. It begins to stir and wake up.

The creature uncurls its massive body. Its serpent head rises on a slender neck. And then another head rises. And another, and another.

"Oh no! Is that the Hydra?" Giganta asks.

"No. It's worse," Wonder Woman replies as they run straight toward the giant snake monster.

"What could be worse than the Hydra?" Giganta asks.

Turn the page.

"The hundred-headed dragon of the Hesperides," Wonder Woman answers.

"And you say you can handle that thing?" Giganta says.

Wonder Woman twirls her golden lasso as she runs toward the snake. She tosses the loop over one of the dragon's heads and pulls the rope tight around the serpent neck. Then Wonder Woman leaps onto its back.

"The Golden Lasso of Truth compels you to obey me!" she says.

"ROAAAAR!" the dragon answers and shakes all of its heads.

Turn to page 96.

"Let's steer clear of those centaurs," Wonder Woman says.

"Why's that?" Giganta asks.

"Based on the myths my mother told me, centaurs can be savage fighters," the Amazon warrior replies. "Even though they look peaceful here in Elysium, we don't want to take any chances with them. We can't afford a delay in finding the cave of Orpheus and the way out of the Underworld."

Wonder Woman and Giganta start to make their way around the centaurs when they see a large shape heading straight toward them. It is Cerberus, the hound of Hades.

"Uh-oh. It looks like Hades has sent his three-headed pet to fetch us back to him," Wonder Woman says.

"What do you mean *us?*" Giganta says and starts to run away from Wonder Woman. "He's not fetching me anywhere!"

Turn the page.

Wonder Woman takes off in the opposite direction. She hopes to confuse Cerberus. He won't be able to choose who to chase. Her plan works. The giant guard dog stops. One head watches as Wonder Woman runs away and another head watches Giganta retreating. The heads yip and bark as if talking to each other. Then Cerberus bounds after Wonder Woman.

The hound of Hades has supernatural speed. He catches up to Wonder Woman. But the Amazon Princess also has amazing speed. She dodges and weaves across the golden Elysian Fields, keeping just ahead of Cerberus.

Cerberus barks at Wonder Woman, but it is not an angry sound.

He sounds happy. He thinks I'm playing with him! Wonder Woman realizes.

As Wonder Woman races over the meadow, she takes her golden lasso and shapes it into a ball. She throws it over Cerberus's three heads.

"Fetch!" Wonder Woman says.

The giant hound barks and chases after the golden ball. He soon returns with it in one of his three mouths. He drops it at Wonder Woman's feet and wags his tail. Cerberus bounces back and forth in front of her as if to say "more."

"You are a slobber machine," Wonder Woman says as she picks up the balled-up lasso dripping with drool. She tosses the ball again and Cerberus races after it.

Turn to page 99.

"I choose to go forward," Wonder Woman decides. She claps her bracelets together with a mighty **BOOOOM!** The shock wave knocks down a bunch of the zombies, but many more surge forward to attack her.

Giganta grows to a tremendous height and stomps on a horde of the evil dead. They wriggle like worms under her foot, then squirm free and swarm up her leg.

"Ew! Yuck! They're not only cold, they're slimy!" Giganta says.

"They are also relentless," Wonder Woman says as she throws zombies off her back. "We could fight them forever. But I have other places to be."

Wonder Woman spreads out her arms and starts to spin. She goes faster and faster, using her Amazon speed until she forms a vortex.

Wonder Woman spins like a tornado. The zombie ghouls get sucked up like dead twigs. The ghouls clutching Giganta are pulled in too.

Turn the page.

Then Wonder Woman suddenly stops spinning. The zombies go flying in all directions. None of them return to renew the battle.

"I must thank The Flash for teaching me that little trick," Wonder Woman says.

Wonder Woman and Giganta trek across the wide meadow, which blooms with tall, white asphodel flowers. They are the only plants growing as far as the eye can see. The pale petals glow in the gloomy light like ghosts.

"This place is sort of pretty once you get past the attacking zombie hordes," Giganta says.

"You must not let your guard down for even a moment," Wonder Woman warns. "The Fields of Asphodel are not as famous as Tartarus or Elysium, but all the realms ruled by Hades have their dangers."

"I don't know much about Greek mythology, but I remember the story about Orpheus escaping the Underworld," Giganta says. "If he can do it, so can we."

"So did Hercules. But he and Orpheus had Hades's permission to leave. We don't," Wonder Woman says. "But you have a point, Giganta. If they found a way out of the Underworld, so can we."

"You're the expert on Greek mythology. How did they do it?" Giganta asks.

"The myths aren't clear about that. I think Hades made sure it was kept secret," Wonder Woman says. "But the entrance to the Underworld is usually a cave. It would make sense if the exit was the same thing."

Turn to page 103.

"You will carry us away from the Stymphalian Birds," Wonder Woman commands the dragon. "Giganta! Hop aboard!"

Giganta leaps onto the monster's back. It slithers swiftly across the rocky ground at amazing speed. The birds are soon left far behind them.

"Typhon said the exit from the Underworld was at the edge of Tartarus. Dragon, take us there," Wonder Woman says.

The giant serpent slithers toward a set of low hills in the distance. They soon come to a building that looks like an ancient Greek temple. It is built into the side of the hill. Wonder Woman and Giganta slide off the dragon's back and walk into the temple. It is not empty. Something very large fills the interior.

"Not another monster!" Giganta groans.

"I am not a monster. I am Arachne, Queen of the Spiders," says the half-woman, half-spider.

Arachne hangs in the middle of a giant web. Wonder Woman can see the exit behind it.

"We have no reason to fight you," Wonder Woman says. "Let us pass, Arachne."

"Why should I?" Arachne asks.

"Because I'll tie your legs in knots if you don't," Giganta says and grows as large as Arachne.

"Now, now, Giganta. Give Arachne a chance," Wonder Woman says. She takes off her tiara and taps its sharp, pointed tip with her finger. Then she looks at the spider's web. "We don't want to fight you, Arachne, but we will."

"You would cut my *web* . . ." Arachne moans. "You may pass."

The Queen of the Spiders retreats. Her web lifts. Wonder Woman and Giganta walk safely toward the exit.

"Whew! My bluff worked," says Wonder Woman.

Turn the page.

"What. You weren't going to cut her web?" Giganta asks.

"No. That would be mean. Arachne is . . . I mean was . . . a gifted weaver," Wonder Woman explains. "She bragged that her skills were better than those of Athena and got turned into a spider because of it. Arachne has been punished enough."

"Those Greek gods of yours sure had a lot of imagination when it came to punishment," Giganta says. "Jail seems tame in comparison."

"I'm glad you think so," Wonder Woman says. "That's where you're going when we get home."

THE END

To follow another path, turn to page 11.

"Let's go find Giganta," Wonder Woman tells Cerberus when the hound returns. "Fetch Giganta!"

YIP! YIP! Cerberus sniffs the air and then bounds away. Wonder Woman runs after him. She soon sees Giganta in the distance.

"I'll race you!" Wonder Woman says to the hound and takes off at full Amazon speed.

Giganta doesn't know what to make of the sight of Wonder Woman and Cerberus racing toward her. Her first instinct is to flee. Giganta grows to an enormous size and starts running. Her strides take her quickly across the fields. But she is no match for Wonder Woman's speed.

"Slow down, Giganta! Cerberus is our friend!" Wonder Woman says.

Cerberus barks and bounces playfully around Giganta's ankles.

"Are you kidding? That mutt brought us here in the first place," Giganta says. But she slows down a little.

Turn the page.

"He just wants someone to play with. I don't think Hades is the type to play fetch," Wonder Woman says. "Watch!"

Wonder Woman tosses the balled-up lasso, and Cerberus races after it. Giganta slows to a trot. She stops running when she sees Cerberus return with the golden ball.

"Good boy!" Wonder Woman says and scratches the hound behind the ears on one of his heads.

Giganta shrinks down to fifteen feet and ruffles one of Cerberus's other heads.

"I like dogs," Giganta says.

Wonder Woman and Giganta continue to play with Cerberus as they make their way to the cave of Orpheus. When they reach the opening, they are sad to say goodbye to the hound of Hades. Giganta gives Cerberus a huge hug around all three necks. Wonder Woman pats each forehead. Cerberus whines. He knows they must leave him.

Turn to page 102.

"I never thought I would miss a giant, three-headed dog, but I already do," Giganta says as she and Wonder Woman enter the cave.

"So do I," Wonder Woman says. "Of course, now that we know about Orpheus's cave, we could always come back to the Underworld."

Wonder Woman and Giganta look at each other. Then they say as one:

"Nah."

THE END

To follow another path, turn to page 11.

Giganta uses her great height to look out across the meadow.

"Um, I see something that looks like a cave," Giganta says. "It could be the way out of here!"

Giganta starts to run across the meadow on giant legs, leaving Wonder Woman behind.

"So much for 'we'," Wonder Woman says.

Wonder Woman uses her Amazon speed to catch up with Giganta. As she pulls within a few strides, the villain stops in front of a cave opening. But instead of rushing in, Giganta stands as still as a stone statue. Wonder Woman sees why.

"Medusa!" Wonder Woman says.

Just inside the cave stands the shadowy shape of a tall woman. Snakes grow out of her head instead of hair. The creatures twist and writhe at the sight of Wonder Woman.

HISSS! HISSS!

Turn the page.

Wonder Woman takes extra care not to look at the eyes of Medusa. She knows the monster's gaze is famous for turning people to stone. *But does Giganta?* the hero wonders.

Wonder Woman quickly turns to look at Giganta. To her great relief, the villain is frozen in fear, not turned to stone.

"Shut your eyes, Giganta," Wonder Woman says. "Don't look at Medusa. And don't move."

Giganta obeys. Then Wonder Woman slides her golden tiara down from her forehead to cover her eyes.

Using her tiara as a blindfold, Wonder Woman enters the cave. Medusa attacks, but the hero hears the hissing snakes and swiftly dodges. She uses the sound to guide her in battle against Medusa.

WHACK! WHACK!

Wonder Woman smacks Medusa with her bracelets at Amazon speed. Medusa is forced to defend herself instead of attacking her opponent.

At last, Wonder Woman's combat skills are too much for Medusa. She slithers away.

"It's safe, Giganta," Wonder Woman says.

"Safe?!" Giganta cries. "This whole place is a death trap."

"Then the sooner we leave the better. I see a light at the back of the cave. It might be coming from the Upper World," Wonder Woman says.

"Might?" Giganta asks nervously. "Um, in that case you can lead the way."

THE END

To follow another path, turn to page 11.

AUTHOR

Laurie S. Sutton has been reading comics since she was
a kid. She grew up to become an editor for Marvel, DC
Comics, Starblaze, and Tekno Comics. She has written
Adam Strange for DC, *Star Trek: Voyager* for Marvel, plus
Star Trek: Deep Space Nine and *Witch Hunter* for Malibu
Comics. There are long boxes of comics in her closet
where there should be clothing and shoes. Laurie has
lived all over the world, and currently resides in Florida.

ILLUSTRATOR

Omar Lozano lives in Monterrey, Mexico. He has always
been crazy for illustration and is constantly on the
lookout for awesome things to draw. In his free time, he
watches lots of movies, reads fantasy and sci-fi books,
and draws! Omar has worked for Marvel, DC, IDW,
Capstone, and several other publishing companies.

GLOSSARY

archery (AR-chuh-ree)—the sport of shooting at targets using a bow and arrow

banish (BAN-ish)—to send away forever

barren (BA-ruhn)—producing little or no plant life

captivating (KAP-ti-vay-ting)—holding one's full attention

eternal (i-TUR-nuhl)—a seemingly endless time period

javelin (JAV-uh-luhn)—a light, metal spear that is thrown for distance in a track-and-field event

mortal (MOR-tuhl)—human, referring to a being who will eventually die

myth (MITH)—a story from ancient times

mythology (mi-THOL-uh-jee)—a collection of myths

platinum (PLAT-uh-nuhm)—a precious silvery-white metal often used in jewelry

realm (RELM)—kingdom

sapling (SAP-ling)—a young tree

scholar (SKOL-ur)—a person who has done advanced study in a special field

serpent (SUR-puhnt)—a snake

spar (SPAHR)—to practice fighting

tapestry (TAP-uh-stree)—a heavy piece of cloth with pictures or patterns woven into it

GIGANTA

Occupation:
Criminal

Base:
Metropolis

Height:
6 feet 6 inches
or taller

Weight:
Varies

Eyes:
Blue

Hair:
Red

Powers/Abilities:
Size-shifting, super-strength, and invulnerability. As
a giant she is almost as strong as Wonder Woman.

Giganta's origin connects back to the villain Gorilla Grodd. The gorilla mastermind created Giganta by changing an ape into a human woman. In the process, he gave her the power to increase her size to towering heights—and her strength along with it. For a time, Giganta partnered with Grodd. She was even the most loyal member of his Secret Society, until a run-in with the Justice League landed her in jail. By the time Giganta got out, another super-villain had taken her place beside Grodd, and Giganta's feelings toward him soured. Now the size-changing super-villain typically works alone, and her criminal capers often land her in the crosshairs of Wonder Woman.

- The Secret Society isn't the only villainous organization Giganta has joined. She once served as a member of the Legion of Doom. In an interesting twist of fate, she even helped the Legion defend Earth against an invasion by the super-villain Darkseid.

- Giganta is one of Wonder Woman's most destructive enemies. Her enormous size and super-strength make it nearly impossible for her not to crush cars, damage buildings, and topple bridges while committing crimes. Wherever she goes, Giganta leaves a path of destruction in her wake.

- Although Giganta is difficult to stop, Wonder Woman's superpowers often give her the edge in battle. The Amazon Princess relies on her super-strength when going toe to toe with the powerful giantess. And her ability to fly is particularly handy whenever Giganta grows to new heights.

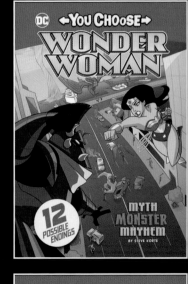

THE FUN DOESN'T STOP HERE!

DISCOVER MORE AT...
www.CAPSTONEKIDS.com